Will You Be My Friend?

Read more books in this series:

My Family's Fantastic!

Tell Us A Bedtime Story

WILL YOU BE MY FRIEND?
A PICTURE CORGI BOOK 978 0 552 57610 9
Published in Great Britain in 2012
by Picture Corgi, an imprint of Random House Children's Publishers UK
A Random House Group Company
This edition published 2012

3 5 7 9 10 8 6 4

Copyright © Random House Children's Books, 2012
Illustrated by Julia Seal
The right of Julia Seal to be identified as the illustrator of this work has
been asserted in accordance with the Copyright, Designs and Patents Act 1988.
Picture Corgi Books are published by Random House Children's Publishers UK,
61–63 Uxbridge Road, London W5 5SA
www.randomhousechildrens.co.uk
www.randomhouse.co.uk
Addresses for companies within The Random House Group Limited can be found at:
www.randomhouse.co.uk/offices.htm
THE RANDOM HOUSE GROUP Limited Reg. No. 954009
A CIP catalogue record for this book is available from the British Library.
Printed in China

Will You Be My Friend?

Illustrated by Julia Seal

Picture Corgi

Ben had been playing with Mr Ted all day,
but now Mr Ted was grumpy.

"Don't you want to be my friend anymore, Mr Ted?"
asked Ben. But Mr Ted said nothing.

Ben built a beautiful castle with building blocks.

But nobody wanted to come and live in it.

He made a den out of cushions and Dad's jumpers.

But nobody wanted to play in it.

Even Bumble the cat was in an unfriendly mood.

So Ben went to talk to his big brother, Stephen.
Stephen was very, very sleepy, but he gave Ben
a rather good idea . . .

As his clever big brother suggested, Ben went to talk to Edwina, his big sister's goldfish.

"Will you be my friend?" he whispered.

Edwina stared at Ben for a little while,
but then she swam off.

So Ben went to talk to his Mum and Dad.
"No one wants to play with me," he said sadly.

"Let's go to the park and see if some of your friends are there," said Mum.

But when they got to the playground there was no one Ben knew.

"Why don't you go and say hello to one of the children?" suggested Mum. "I'm sure they would love to play."

But the playground seemed very big and scary. Would anybody let Ben join in?

He went and talked to a little boy.
"Will you be my friend?" Ben asked quietly.

"No, sorry," said the boy. "I'm quite busy with
these marbles, thank you."

So Ben asked a little girl, "Will you be my friend?"

"No, sorry," said the girl. "I don't like boys."

Everyone seemed to be too busy to play, or
they had lots of friends already.

A group of mean boys laughed at Ben when he asked
if he could join in their game.

Ben went and stood on his own. He felt miserable.
He looked up at a little lonely bird sitting in a tree.
"Will **you** be my friend?" he asked.

But the bird flew away.

All of a sudden, Ben saw a little girl peeking
out from behind the tree.

"Hello," said the little girl, shyly. "I'm Mia."
"Hello, I'm Ben," said Ben.
"Mr Monks is in a very bad mood today," said Mia.
"But maybe we could play together?"

Ben introduced Mr Ted to Mr Monks.
"I think they're going to be friends," said Ben.

Ben smiled at Mia, and Mia smiled at Ben.
And together they ran to play in the sandpit.

From that day on, Ben and Mia often met in
the park with Mr Ted and Mr Monks.
And they quickly made lots of new friends . . .

And whenever anyone asked,
"Will you be my friend?"
they all said . . .

"Yes!
We'll be your friends!"